THE SABBATH LION

More than Israel has kept the Sabbath,
the Sabbath has kept Israel.

— Ahad Ha'am

THE SABBATH LION

A Jewish Folktale from Algeria

Retold by Howard Schwartz and Barbara Rush

Illustrated by Stephen Fieser

HarperCollins*Publishers*

L ONG AGO, in the faraway city of Algiers, there lived a Jewish widow and her seven children. She had to work from dawn until dark to feed her large family. The woman's eldest son, Yosef, was only ten years old, but he tried to help his mother as much as he could.

Every day, except Saturday, Yosef went to the marketplace to sweep the shopkeepers' stalls and keep their baskets full of fresh fruits and vegetables. Because he was such a good worker, the shopkeepers gave Yosef a small bag of rice, a few oranges, and, every now and then, nuts and dates to take home to his family.

YOUNG YOSEF rested only on the Sabbath. How he loved and honored this holy day! On Friday evenings, his mother lit the Sabbath candles and said a blessing. Then Yosef, holding his glass high, said the blessing over the wine. And raising the challah, a braided loaf that his mother baked on Friday mornings, he said the blessing over this special Sabbath bread. After that, Yosef and all the children turned to the door and sang a song welcoming the Sabbath Queen: "Come, O Sabbath Queen, and bring peace and blessing on thy wing!" Then they had their finest meal of the week, with candles glowing brightly around them.

On Saturday mornings, Yosef and his brothers walked to the synagogue to pray. Yosef did not travel or do any work on the Sabbath, because it was forbidden. And he knew that a peaceful Sabbath gave him the strength to work hard the rest of the week.

ONE DAY, when Yosef was working in the market, he saw a stranger speaking to one of the shopkeepers. He overheard the man ask where a certain family could be found. Yosef ran over. "That's my family!" he cried. "Let me lead you to my house." And when they arrived there, the stranger handed Yosef's mother a letter. Then he bowed and left.

Yosef's mother read the letter and turned pale.

"What's the matter, Mother?" the children asked.

Their mother answered, "Strange news has come our way. It seems that your father had an uncle who lived in the city of Cairo, in the land of Egypt. And when he died, there was no one to leave his fortune to, so he left it to us." Hearing this, the children gasped—soon they would have money for food and maybe even a few new clothes!

YET THEIR MOTHER still looked worried. "The money would be a great blessing," she said, "but I would have to travel all the way to Egypt to claim it. How can I take seven young children on such a long journey? I have no one to leave you with, and you're too young to be left alone."

"Please, Mother," said Yosef, "let me go to Cairo to get it!"

"But Yosef, you are too young. The sun is very hot. Wild animals live in the desert. No, no, no, it would not be safe for you to cross the desert."

"Please, Mother," begged Yosef, "have faith in God. Has He not sent us a great blessing? We must not ignore it."

When Yosef's mother saw how strong her son's faith was, she finally agreed to let him go. But it was very expensive to travel across the desert, for he must join a caravan. Yosef's mother emptied all the hidden boxes in which she had been saving money for Passover and found just enough for the journey. Then she rushed out of the house to pay the leader of the caravan for Yosef's trip.

ECAUSE YOSEF would not travel on the Sabbath, she asked the caravan leader if he would agree to rest on the Sabbath day. But the leader said, "It is dangerous to rest in the hot desert, where wild animals attack. If you want us to stop on your Sabbath, you will have to pay more." And the man named a large sum of money.

Yosef's mother was shocked. She had already given him all her savings. What else could she do? So the poor woman sold her golden wedding ring, the only valuable possession she had left. Then she gave the money to the leader of the caravan in exchange for his promise to rest on the Sabbath.

The caravan left Algiers early Sunday morning. In his sack Yosef carried a letter from his mother, explaining that she had sent her son to collect the family's inheritance. He also took a pouch with candles, a small bottle of wine, a wine cup, and a little challah his mother had baked, so he could celebrate the Sabbath even when he was far from home. So too did he bring a wooden spice box and a candle with many wicks for the blessings at the end of the Sabbath.

T HE CARAVAN TRUDGED through the vast desert. Everywhere Yosef looked, he saw sand and only sand. The days passed slowly. The camels walked carefully across the burning sands, and the caravan would rest only when it was almost dark. Then Yosef would climb down from his camel and help the men set up tents for the night and gather brush for the campfire. And, at the first sight of dawn, the caravan would be once again on its way.

SIX LONG DAYS passed, and finally it was Friday afternoon, almost the eve of the Sabbath. Yosef went to the leader of the caravan to remind him of their agreement.

"What agreement?" the man asked, much to Yosef's dismay. "I don't know of any agreement."

"Why, my mother sold her wedding ring and paid you to stop on the Sabbath! You promised!" shouted Yosef, beginning to cry.

The leader of the caravan stared boldly into Yosef's eyes.

"We are going on," he said, "for there is still a bit of daylight left and tomorrow we will ride all day. If you want to come with us, come! If not, stay here by yourself!"

Yosef looked up and saw that before long, the sun would be setting, and he knew that he had to prepare for the Sabbath.

"Well, are you coming?" asked the caravan leader, his voice nasty and impatient.

Poor Yosef wanted to continue with the caravan, where he would be safe. But no matter what the dangers were, even if he were to be lost in the desert forever, Yosef could never disobey the laws of the Sabbath. And so his answer to the leader was firm: "No, I'm not coming. Go on without me. I must stay behind." And as the camels of the caravan left, he watched them disappear into the distance until he could see nothing but a cloud of dust.

THE SUN was setting and the Sabbath was about to begin. Yosef knew that he must light the campfire quickly before the sun had set, and that he must put enough brush on the fire to burn through the night. This he did, and then, as it grew dark, he sat down and sang his song to the Sabbath Queen: "Come, O Sabbath Queen, and bring peace and blessing on thy wing."

There Yosef sat, surrounded by the desert, without even a tree for shelter, with only the fire to keep wild animals away. He was afraid, so he closed his eyes and prayed with all his heart. But when he opened them, he saw something that made him tremble. For there in the distance was a huge lion, moving swiftly in his direction.

As the lion came closer, Yosef froze in terror, certain that his life was about to end. But when the lion was so close that Yosef could almost touch it, the huge beast quietly lay down at his feet. Yosef was afraid that the lion would pounce on him, but when it turned its head, Yosef saw that its eyes were kind.

T HEN HE OPENED his pouch and took out the candles, the challah, the wine, and the wine cup. He lit the candles in the fire, and in a clear voice he recited all the blessings. And as he did so, he was filled with a feeling of peace, as if he were at home, celebrating the Sabbath with his mother and his brothers and sisters. Soon afterward, he fell asleep.

Yosef awoke at dawn, and there was the lion, still watching over him. The hours of the day passed. Yosef sang Sabbath songs and recited Sabbath prayers. He felt as calm and peaceful as he had the night before. And never once during all that time did the lion move from where it lay. Yosef was glad that he was not alone, and he was thankful for the company of his Sabbath friend.

At last the sun set, and Yosef took out his wooden spice box, the candle with many wicks, and a cup of wine, and he said the special prayers for the end of the Sabbath. All this time the lion seemed to listen patiently. And then, when the prayers were over, the lion's kind eyes looked into Yosef's. It was then that the boy understood what had happened: The Sabbath Queen had sent the lion as a wonderful present to protect him.

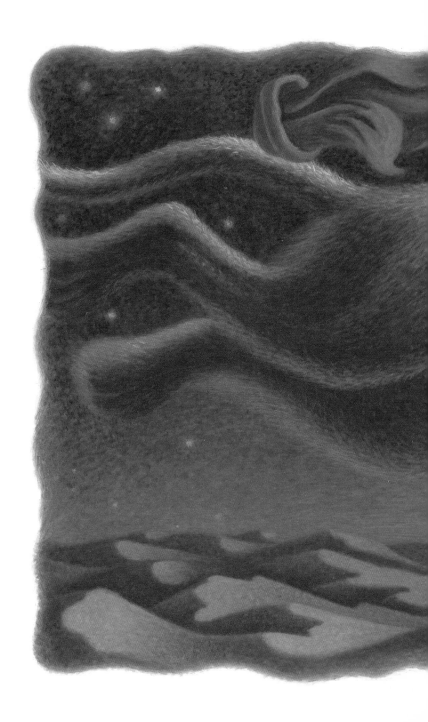

H E STROKED the lion's mane and put his arms around its neck. The lion brushed its tail against its back, which was the lion's way of telling Yosef that it wanted him to mount. And no sooner did Yosef do so than the lion raced off across the desert, with the boy clinging to its mane, while the moon and the stars lit their way.

Soon they arrived at an oasis, where there were lush fig trees and a clear freshwater pool. After a long, cool drink and a meal of figs, Yosef felt much better. He said a prayer of thanks and then he and the lion set off again.

EARLY SUNDAY MORNING, Yosef saw a cloud of dust in the distance. It was the caravan! The lion had caught up with it in only one night.

Now when the travelers saw a great lion with someone riding on it, they were terrified. They quickly threw themselves down before Yosef, afraid the lion would devour them all.

The caravan leader watched in fear as the lion brought Yosef directly to him. In a shaky voice, he welcomed Yosef back and asked him to be the new leader. He also gave back every penny Yosef's mother had paid him, and never again did he break a promise as long as he lived.

S O IT WAS that Yosef and the Sabbath lion led the caravan all the rest of the way to Cairo. There they rode through the narrow streets, where people screamed and scattered this way and that, running from the huge beast coming toward them.

Soon the lion, with the boy still on its back, arrived at the office where Yosef was to collect the money. From their hiding places, everyone watched in amazement as the lion stood guard and Yosef went inside. A short time later, clutching two bags of silver coins, he came out, jumped on the lion's back, and rode away.

YOSEF AND THE LION sped through the desert once more. And before long Yosef saw the walled city of Algiers, where his mother, brothers, and sisters awaited him. Suddenly the lion stopped. Yosef knew that the lion had completed its task. The time had come to bid his friend good-bye. He petted the lion and hugged it hard. The lion nodded as it rubbed against Yosef. Then it ran off into the desert and disappeared. With one last look behind him, Yosef passed through the gates of the city and hurried down the streets of Algiers to his home.

WHEN YOSEF'S FAMILY saw that he was home unharmed, they said prayers of thanks. And now that he had completed his task, the family could buy food and clothing and, yes, even a silver spice box for the closing of the Sabbath. And every Sabbath after that, the children begged Yosef to tell them his story, and he gladly did. For never did a Sabbath pass that he did not remember the Sabbath Queen and the wonderful lion she sent to him.

For Shira, Nathan, and Miriam —*H.S.*
For Simha and Don — *B.R.*
For Cherie — *S.F.*

COMMENTARY

The Jewish Sabbath celebrates the idea of resting after a hard week's work. Everyone rests on the Sabbath: grown-ups, children, and animals, too.

The Sabbath begins at sunset on Friday night, when children and grown-ups, wearing their best clothes, sing a song of welcome to the Sabbath Queen. In Jewish lore the spirit of the Sabbath is often identified as the Sabbath Queen.

Also on Friday night, at the beginning of Sabbath, the mother lights candles and recites a blessing to thank God for these lights. Then the father says a special prayer called the *Kiddush*, thanking God for wine to drink. The family eats a special braided bread called *challah* and eats other tasty foods.

On Saturday night, at the end of Sabbath, there is another beautiful ceremony called *Havdalah*. A special candle is lit and blessings are said over the lights, wine, and special fragrant spices. After the blessings are said, the Sabbath is over.

The story of the Sabbath Lion is told by Jews in North Africa and in other places such as Iran and Bukhara. This version was collected by A. Rabi from Avner Azolai and is found in *Avotanu Sippru*, edited by Moshe Rabi, published in Jerusalem in 1975. It is number 6432 in the Israel Folktale Archives.

The Sabbath Lion: A Jewish Folktale from Algeria
Text copyright © 1992 by Howard Schwartz and Barbara Rush
Illustrations copyright © 1992 by Stephen Carl Fieser
Printed in the U.S.A. All rights reserved.
Typography by Al Cetta
2 3 4 5 6 7 8 9 10

Library of Congress Cataloging-in-Publication Data
Schwartz, Howard, date
     The Sabbath lion : a Jewish folktale from Algeria / retold by Howard
Schwartz and Barbara Rush ; illustrated by Stephen Fieser.
         p.   cm.
     Summary: Because of Yosef's devotion to honoring the Sabbath, he is given special
protection by a great lion during a dangerous journey through the desert.
     ISBN 0-06-020853-8. — ISBN 0-06-020854-6 (lib. bdg.)
     [1. Folklore—Jewish.   2. Folklore—Algeria.   3. Sabbath—Folklore.]
I. Rush, Barbara.   II. Fieser, Stephen, ill.   III. Title.
PZ8.I.S4Sab   1992   91-35766
398.2—dc20   CIP
[E]   AC